Hey Khari and Kalia,

This book is dedicated to you. Your mother wanted me to tell you that you are a big part of her inspiration and that she loves you with all of her heart.

Published by
Worlds To Discover, LLC.

Created by Jacquitta A. McManus

Written by Jacquitta A. McManus
Illustrations by Jacquitta A. McManus & Brian Hardison

ISBN: 978-0-9828027-5-5

For information regarding permission, write
Worlds To Discover, LLC.
P.O. Box 5425
Douglasville, GA 30154

WorldsToDiscover.com

Talee and the fallen object

By Jacquitta A. McManus

Worlds To Discover, LLC.

Table of Contents

1
Talee

Hello everyone. My name is Talee. It's spelled T-A-L-E-E and it is pronounced (TAH-Lee).

I just came in from outside. The sun is out and the air feels warm. Can you feel it?

Today, I want to tell you a story I wrote about one of my GREAT adventures.

It's a real story. Really!

It happened a couple of weeks ago.

Oh, but first I should tell you about me.

The first thing you should know is that I'm eight.

Yep! Eight and I love to read and write—especially about great adventures. My favorites are treasure hunts.

My favorite colors are purple and yellow and I wear them every day. Right now I'm wearing my purple jumpsuit, yellow socks and purple boots with yellow on them. I love my boots.

My favorite food is wild puffy muffins--the yellow ones with the pink tops as big as my hand.

The puffier, the pinker, the bigger, the better is what I always say.

My mom makes them for me every weekend and they're the best.

Mm-mmm!

There's nothing better than a wild puffy muffin for breakfast.

I live on the planet Gala. It's a really cool place to live.

I think you'd like it here too.

It's always warm and it doesn't rain much, which is good since I don't like rain. I don't like being wet unless I'm going swimming. Then I don't mind. But we don't go swimming that much.

Gala has two moons; one is big and blue and one is small and white.

And both moons orbit together, so when you see one you see the other.

I love looking up at the sky and seeing the moons.

I call them wishing moons and every night

I look out my window and make a wish before I go to bed.

I would tell you what my last wish was for, but then it might not come true so I'll have to keep that a secret for now. But it was a really good wish.

To me Gala is the best planet ever. There's so much amazing stuff here, like…the land floats.

Yep, *floats.*

Great, right?

When I look out my window I see lots of other floating landmasses just like the one I live on. Most of them are small and just have one house, a small yard and a house for Calpas on them.

Some of the big ones have tall buildings on them, but I don't visit them much.

The ones that are too small for a house are left alone. My dad says they're too small to build on. I guess that makes sense.

I suspect now you're wondering what a Calpa is and how we get around if all the land floats in separate pieces.

That's easy.

Calpas fly, and we ride on them.

Calpas are big friendly flying animals. The have large, pretty wings and they're really cute. Everybody has at least one. Sometimes two. If the family is big they have three or even more.

We only have two but there are only three of us. I don't have a brother or a sister. Sometimes I wish I did.

Our Calpas are named Bett and Ran.

Bett is yellow with gray feet and pink in her wings. Ran is gray and white and her wings also have pink in them.

And they're big. I mean *really* big. They're taller than me.

If I want to get on one of them I have to get them to lie down or use a ladder, but most times they just lie down and let me climb on when I ask.

I love riding a Calpa because I love flying.

I love it when they fly fast and the wind rushes by my face and pushes my hair back. It's a great feeling.

But enough about me. Let's get back to my great adventure.

2
Treasure

It started early one Saturday morning. I had nothing to do. I mean nothing at all.

I had eaten all of my puffy muffins and drank all of my juice. I had some purple juice that my mom had made from purple berries. She put white cream on top, too. Yummy!

Mom and dad were in the living room reading the morning paper and none of my friends were out playing, which I didn't understand because it was such a pretty day.

So I went to my room and picked one of my favorite Captain Jewel books, *Captain Jewel and the Lost City Treasure,* from a stack on the floor and sat down on my bed to read.

It was a good book so it didn't take me long to get through the first two chapters.

Captain Jewel had just gotten news that a bag of treasure was hidden in a lost city and she only had three days to find it, which I knew wouldn't be hard for Captain Jewel because she always found her treasure.

Anyway, just when I started reading the third chapter I saw a mail flyer go by outside the window.

Of course, there's nothing unusual

about that. Mail flyers deliver the mail every morning. But this time something had fallen out of the mail flyer's bag.

I jumped out of my bed to get a better look. My book fell on the floor and I didn't even care because I *had* to see what was falling through the air.

I ran to my window and saw a round object falling through the air very fast.

It landed on a small floating landmass, and when it hit the ground smoke started rising from where it had landed.

I tried to guess what it was, thinking maybe it was a rock, a ball, a bag of treasure.

Yes! *A bag of treasure!* It had to be.

For a moment I stood there looking and thinking about the treasure. The more I looked the more I wanted that bag.

I had to go get it, so I went to our Calpas' house.

Bett and Ran were asleep. I woke them up anyway, and they didn't like that at all.

They both growled at me.

Then Bett turned to face me and said in a low, sleepy voice, "What do you want, girl?"

I took a deep breath and looked her in the eyes just like Captain Jewel would do.

"I need your help," I said in my most

confident voice. "There's a bag of treasure on one of the small landmasses and I want to go get it. Will you to take me?"

"Go back home," said Bett. "There's no bag of treasure."

"Yes, go back home," repeated Ran before a big yawn.

"No! I saw it fall from a mail flyer just now." I said.

"Then your eyes are playing tricks on you," said Bett.

"Tricks," repeated Ran.

"No they're not. I saw it."

Bett yawned and laid back down and so did Ran.

They didn't believe me and I knew it, but I didn't know how to change their minds.

So I laid down on Bett's side.

I could feel her breathing. My whole body moved up and down with her every breath.

After a few seconds I rubbed Bett's head and she purred.

Then I remembered that they like it when you talk really nicely to them.

So I said. "Please Bett, just take me to see? If there's nothing there we can come right back. I promise."

"Maybe tomorrow," she said, closing her eyes. "I'm very tired. Tomorrow would be better."

"But please, Bett?" I said again.

But Bett didn't pay me any attention. She just yawned and went back to her nap.

This of course made me very mad. I wanted that bag of treasure and I wanted to go get it *now.*

So I said to Bett in my biggest voice, "I order you to take me to the landmass."

It's something Captain Jewel would

do when she needed someone to take her somewhere and they wouldn't listen.

Bett looked up at me.

"Go. Home." She said.

"But *please* Bett," I said in a very nice voice again. "Just please take me."

Then I started climbing on Bett's back. I grabbed her harness and before I could even get all the way on she took off through the air.

Oh, no!

Bett flew fast and I held on tight to her harness.

The wind rushed by my face and my hair blew back.

I saw the floating landmass with the bag of treasure and I told Bett to turn.

I was on my way to find the treasure.

3

Fallen Object

When Bett landed I lost my grip and fell.

"Ah!" I said as I hit the ground hard.

I turned to Bett to see how she was doing and found that she had gone back to sleep.

After taking in a deep breath I got up and brushed myself off.

Then I saw the dust clouds and the big hole right in front of me, and I started smiling.

The bag of treasure!

I crawled over to the hole and looked inside. I could see the round object that had fallen from the sky.

All I had to do was climb down and get it.

After looking around, I began climbing down the big hole. It was easy.

Once I was at the bottom I got a better

look at the fallen object and I could tell it wasn't a bag of treasure.

Boy was I *upset* about that.

Instead, it was an egg. A brown egg with white spots all over it.

It was cracked and the creature inside was looking at me through the crack.

I got so excited! I crawled up to the egg and began to rub it. After rubbing the shell a couple of times, it broke open and a baby Calpa *popped* out.

"Oh!" I said as the Calpa looked up at me. It was so cute.

The baby Calpa started jumping around making a purring sound.

I giggled as I watched.

Once she calmed down I picked her up

and climbed out of the hole.

Then I woke Bett to take us back home. This time I rode on her back.

When I got home I took the baby Calpa up to my room, where I rubbed her head and named her Nola.

And that's the end of my great adventure. Well, *almost.*

4

Nola

As soon as I took Nola to my room and let her down, she started running everywhere. She knocked over everything, even my stack of Captain Jewel books on the floor.

With all the noise she made, my parents came right up to my room and let me tell you, they were not happy.

Actually, they were very upset.

After I told them where I'd found Nola,

they took her and returned her to the mail station.

And I got in big trouble!

My dad talked to me about how dangerous it was to leave the house without their permission. My mom talked to me about how dangerous it was to ride a Calpa when they were sleepy. "They are very disagreeable when they're sleepy," she said. "And that can be very dangerous."

I also got extra chores for a week and if that wasn't bad enough I was also grounded and couldn't go outside to play with my friends.

My friend Cora had a birthday party and I missed it.

I was so sad about it.

At least my mom let me go and buy Cora

a present and take it to her. I got her a pink floating ball. I think it was her favorite gift.

Oh, I almost forgot to tell you!

Nola's owners went and claimed her and took her home the same day my mom returned her to the mail station.

I didn't think I would ever see her again.

My mom said that she was in good hands and that I shouldn't worry about her, but I did. I worried about her a lot.

Then something great happened. After I finished my punishment I ran into Nola's owners and they let me play with her for a little bit.

Then, not even a week later the owners brought Nola to my house.

I was so happy! Nola ran and jumped into

my arms. I gave her a big hug and rubbed her head.

Then the owners asked me if I would help take care of her. Can you believe that?

They said she needed more attention then they could give her.

I was so excited I started to jump up and down, and after talking to my parents and asking them for their permission, I said yes.

A few weeks later Nola came to live with me and now we're best friends.

She was the best treasure I could ever find, even if she knocks things over and I have to clean them up.

Oh, and the first night Nola stayed with me I finished reading *Captain Jewel and the Lost City Treasure.*

Nola loved it. And I love her.

So, that's it! That's the adventure of Talee and the Fallen Object.

Well, until next time.

Wait, one more thing before you go. Don't forget to make a wish on your wishing moon.

Look for the following at
http://www.WorldsToDiscover.com

Free downloads available at:
http://www.WorldsToDiscover.com

CPSIA information can be obtained
at www.ICGtesting.com
Printed in the USA
LVOW05s1513270917
550280LV00007B/71/P